Hooves or Hands?

Rosie Haine

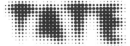

Would you rather be a horse

Or a human?

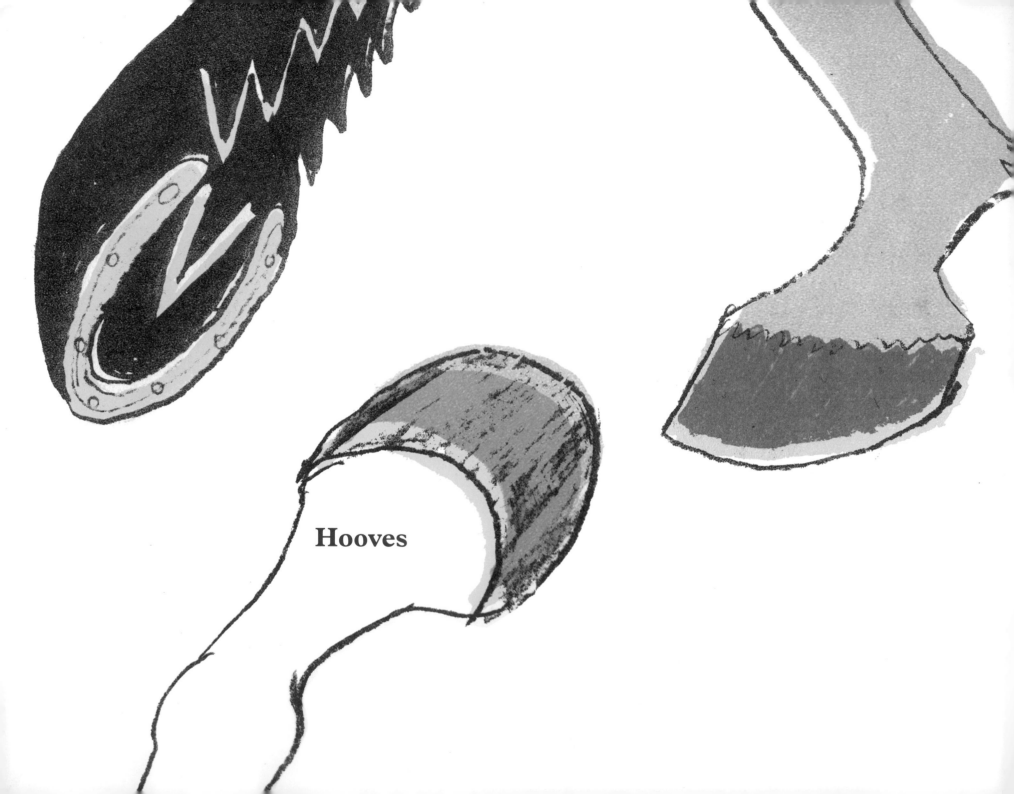

Hooves

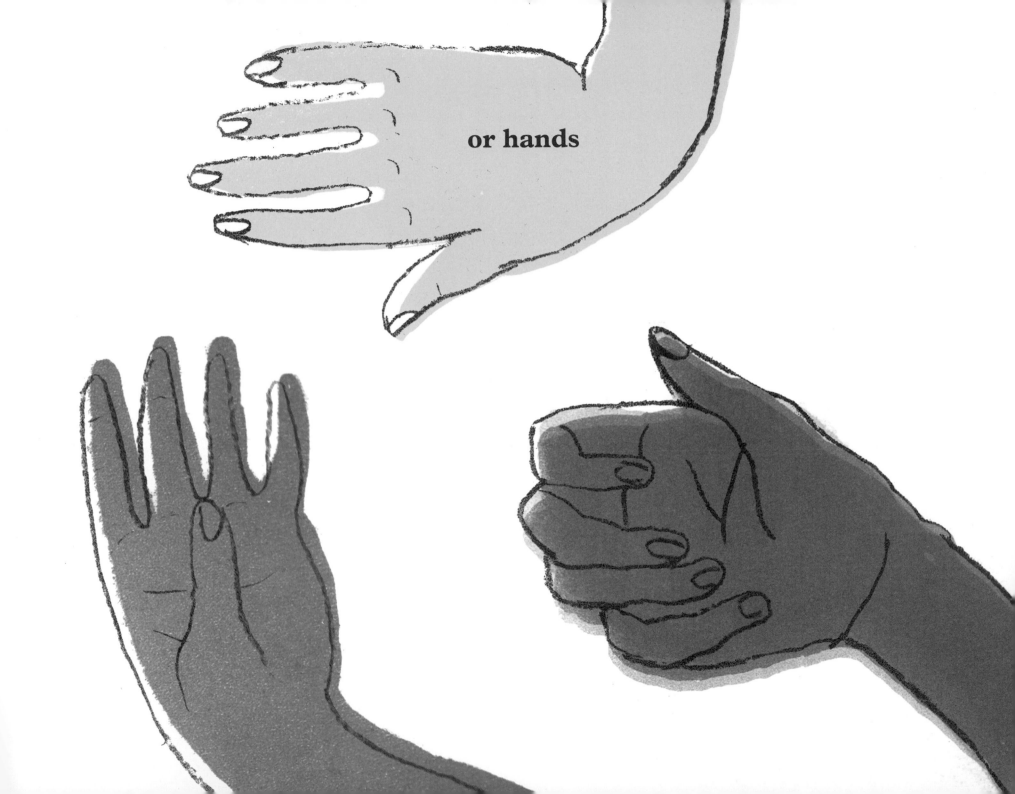

or hands

Four legs

or two

Have a long face or a short face

and have a poo

Gallop or run

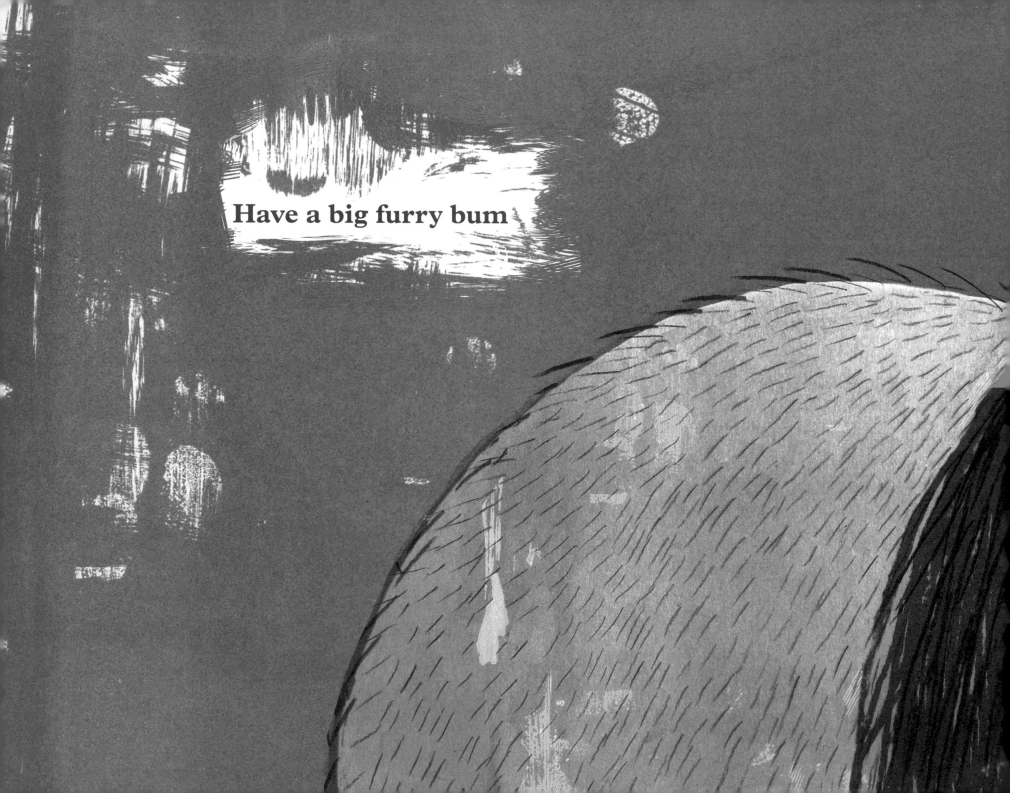

Have a big furry bum

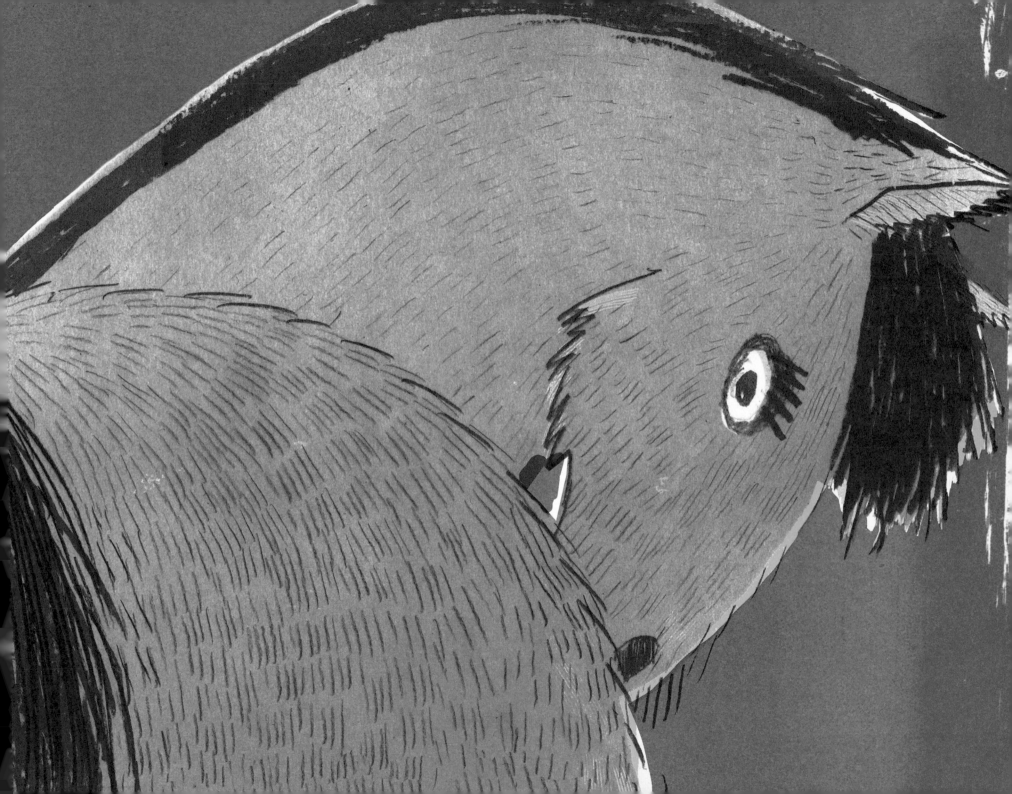

Eat food or hay

Say words or neigh

So would you rather be
a pony or a person?

And if you could choose,
which one is more fun?

Or could you be both?

Whatever you choose

It's up to you!

This book is dedicated to my Grandma Joy Bulford; a wonderful artist who loved horses as much as I do, and who taught me how to draw them.

First published 2021 by order of the Tate Trustees
by Tate Publishing, a division of Tate Enterprises Ltd,
Millbank, London SW1P 4RG
www.tate.org.uk/publishing
Text and illustrations © Rosie Haine 2021

A catalogue record for this book is available from the British Library

ISBN 978-1-84976-758-3

Distributed in the United States and Canada by ABRAMS, New York
Library of Congress Control Number applied for

Colour reproduction by Evergreen Colour Management Ltd
Printed and bound in China by C&C Offset Printing Co., Ltd